THE BAD GUYS

EPISODE 3   EPISODE 4

SCHOLASTIC

Scholastic Children's Books
An imprint of Scholastic Ltd
Euston House, 24 Eversholt Street, London, NW1 1DB, UK
Registered office: Westfield Road, Southam, Warwickshire, CV47 0RA
SCHOLASTIC and associated logos are trademarks and/or
registered trademarks of Scholastic Inc.

Bad Guys in The Furball Strikes Back first published in Australia by Scholastic
Australia, 2016
First published in the UK by Scholastic Ltd, 2018

Bad Guys in Attack of the Zittens first published in Australia by Scholastic
Australia, 2016
First published in the UK by Scholastic Ltd, 2018

This collected edition first published 2018

ISBN 978 1407 19180 5

A CIP catalogue record for this book
is available from the British Library.

Th   hts
and d   used
fict   ad,

AARON BLABEY

THE BAD GUYS

EPISODE 3 THE FURBALL STRIKES BACK

(GOOD)

HEROES OR VILLAINS?

OR

A SPECIAL REPORT BY

1

They are the **MONSTERS** that haunt our darkest nightmares . . .

REENACTMENT

Or ARE they?

Well, not according to THIS chicken . . .

SUNNYSIDE CHICKEN FARM was a terrible place. We spent our whole lives locked in tiny cages. But then that wonderful wolf and his friends—they set us free!

BROOKE

But . . . didn't one of them try to EAT you?

Yes. But he spat me back out again.

IS THIS CHICKEN *CRAZY?*

And Brooke is not the only one to claim that these VILLAINS are actually . . .

HEROES IN DISGUISE!

Every one of the 10,000 chickens set free from Sunnyside has told the same story.

POLICE REPORT

Sunnyside

SHOULD MUTANT SARDINES BE ALLOWED TO WALK THE STREETS?

I thought they were lovely.
Especially the really big chicken.
Or maybe he was a shark.
It was hard to tell . . .

PAT, HOMEMAKER

They inspired me to
follow my dreams.
I'll never forget them.

FIONA, CELEBRITY CHEF

We should all be careful not to judge
others simply by the way they *look*.
Sometimes the scariest-looking creatures
can be the kindest and best of all.

DIANE, SUPREME COURT JUDGE

So, can ALL these chickens be **CRAZY?**

Or are those

HORRIFYING CREATURES

actually . . . trying to do good?

Are they out there doing good deeds?

Or are they **LURKING OUTSIDE YOUR DOOR**, waiting for a chance to show us that they're nothing but a bunch of . . .

. . . BAD GUYS?!

• CHAPTER 1 •

IF YOU GO DOWN TO THE WOODS TODAY . . .

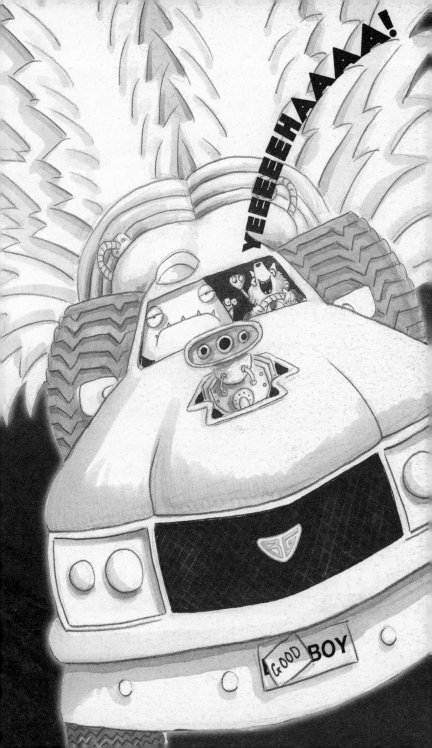

Hey, chico, can you slow down? I don't feel so good . . .

LEGS

IT'S HUG A SPIDER DAY

NO CAN DO, Mr. Piranha. There's NO TIME TO LOSE!

Legs! Are we nearly there?

Yes, Wolfie. According to my satellite signal, we should be seeing the **BULLDOZERS** any minute now . . .

LEGS

IT'S HUG A SPIDER DAY

Great! So, let's go over the plan ONE MORE TIME.

If you tell us the plan one more time, I'm going to bite you on the butt.

WE KNOW THE PLAN!

Hey! Take it easy, Mr. Snake. This is important.

So anyway . . . I got an **ANONYMOUS CALL** telling me that way out here in **THE WOODS**, there's a bunch of **BULLDOZERS** getting ready to smash up the homes of a lot of **CUTE, FURRY ANIMALS**.

And we're here to make sure

THAT DOESN'T HAPPEN.

WE KNOW ALREADY!

Oh man . . . I don't feel good AT ALL . . .

Relax. It's just me.

You are SO good at disguises.

Yeah. I know.

Now, remember, Shark—YOU are a **CUTE FURRY ANIMAL!** It's your job to distract the guys driving the bulldozers while we—

WE KNOW THE PLAN!

Uh-oh. Stop the car . . .

WE'VE BEEN OVER IT A **MILLION** TIMES AND WE **KNOW THE PLAN!**

STOP THE CAR!

SCREEECH!

What's wrong?!

Where are YOU going?

I need to go "number two."

You need to *WHAT*?!

Car travel upsets my tummy.

Are you serious?!
The bulldozers are

**RIGHT
THERE!**

Start without me.
I shouldn't be too long.

Well . . . if you've gotta go . . .

You got it.
If anything moves within
1,000 yards, I'll see it.

All right.
It's time to
be HEROES.

Do you have to say
that EVERY time?

LET'S ROCK!

Hi! I'm an adorable little bunny and I bet you can't catch me!
BOING!
OK, Snake. Wait for the signal . . .

Um . . . guys . . . ?

Um . . . my sensors are picking up something weird about those bulldozers, dudes . . .

Um . . .

. . . is it just me, or is this bulldozer made out of **CARDBOARD** and **STICKY TAPE?**

Hey, that's weird . . .

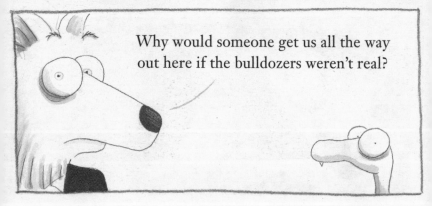

Why would someone get us all the way out here if the bulldozers weren't real?

My car!

LEGS!

Hey, does anyone else think the ground feels weird?

AAARRGGHH!!!

· CHAPTER 2 ·
the LAIR OF
DR. MARMALADE

Wha . . . ?

Well, HELLO, genius.
Nice of you to join us . . .

We're tied up!

Oh, really? Thanks.
WE HADN'T NOTICED!

But who would do this?

Who *wouldn't* do this?
We're **BAD** guys, man.
Guys like us don't get a
happy ending.

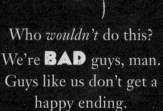

There must have
been a mistake!
**WE'RE
HEROES!**

... SCARE YOU?

Wait a minute! I know you!

You're that cute little
guinea pig from the old
house next to Sunnyside . . .
You're MARMALADE!

That's **DOCTOR** Marmalade to you!

Forgive me.

Allow me to introduce myself . . .

I am
DOCTOR RUPERT MARMALADE!

Welcome to my

HOME!

Hey! I've heard of you!
You're that

BILLIONAIRE MAD SCIENTIST.

Billionaire mad scientist?!
He's a **GUINEA PIG!**

So what?! Just because I'm a
guinea pig, I CAN'T BE A

BILLIONAIRE MAD SCIENTIST?

Oh. Well, no . . . I suppose you could be . . .

Yeah, that's right! And you blew up my awesome car. Why would you do that if you weren't **CRAZY?**

Well, let me think.

Hmmm, yes. Tell me . . . Did you think you could just **BREAK INTO** one of my **CHICKEN FARMS** and steal **10,000 CHICKENS** and I'd just be **COOL WITH THAT?!**

YOUR chicken farm? But you're just a guinea pig!

YOU'RE STILL NOT GETTING IT— I'M A BILLIONAIRE MAD SCIENTIST WHO **OWNS A LOT OF CHICKEN FARMS** AND I'M VERY ANGRY WITH YOU!

Hang on. Are you saying that you blew up our car and strung us up **JUST** because we rescued those chickens?

FINALLY!
Yes, that's right.

But you're *not* mad about all the **BAD** stuff we've done in our lives?

No.

So that means . . .

THE ONLY REASON WE'RE IN THIS MESS IS BECAUSE OF YOUR STUPID OBSESSION WITH **BEING A HERO!**

What? So this is all **MY** fault now?

OF COURSE IT IS! THE ONLY REASON THIS **CRAZY** GUINEA PIG HAS TIED US UP IS BECAUSE YOU **KEEP MAKING US DO GOOD!**

You really want to fight about this NOW?

YOU BET I DO!

THIS RIDICULOUS HERO THING HAS CAUSED US NOTHING BUT TROUBLE AND I'VE HAD ENOUGH!

Hey!

WHAT?!

It's just going to

DESTROY YOU

and help me

TAKE OVER THE ENTIRE WORLD!

HE HE HE HE HE!

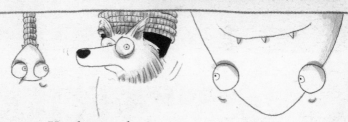

You know what?
I don't think I like that guinea pig.

· CHAPTER 3 ·
DO YOU SEE WHAT I SEE?

Shhh!

¡Ay, caramba! What happened to you?!

I jumped from the car one millisecond before it was **BLOWN TO PIECES BY A LASER CANNON** and then I watched the rest of the gang get **SUCKED INTO THE BOWELS OF THE EARTH.**

Oh. Cool.

WHAT?!

It was a **TRAP**, Mr. Piranha. The bulldozers weren't real. I think someone got us out here deliberately and I think Wolf and the guys have been **CAPTURED!**

My chicos!
But where could they be?!

Look over there . . .

Sunnyside?!
But what's a chicken farm doing out
here in the middle of the woods?

Exactly!
Fishy, don't you think?

Hey! Who are you calling "Fishy"?
And yes, I DO think.

Um . . . OK. Anyway . . .
We need to get inside that
building, and I have a plan . . .

Huh?

Hmmm . . .

BOING!

Give us a kiss.

FAINT!

Wow. He's out cold. You really do freak everyone out, don't you?

Yep. Always have . . .

. . . always . . . will . . .

Hey!

What?

I think . . . I just saw . . .

. . . a **NINJA!**

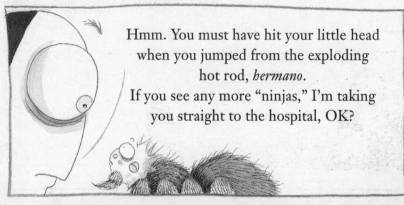

Hmm. You must have hit your little head
when you jumped from the exploding
hot rod, *hermano*.
If you see any more "ninjas," I'm taking
you straight to the hospital, OK?

Because I don't know what
we'll find in here, *chico*. But I'll
promise you one thing . . .

There won't be
any ninjas . . .

• CHAPTER 4 •
the MIND OF A MONSTER

So! Now that I have your attention, I'm going to tell you a little story.

Once upon a time,
there was an itty, bitty guinea pig who got

SICK

of everyone saying how
CUTE and **CUDDLY** he was.

So he decided to do something about it . . .

First of all, he made billions of dollars putting chickens in cages, but somehow that just wasn't enough.

SO! He created a **SECRET WEAPON** that would make sure **NO ONE EVER** called him **CUTE** and **CUDDLY** again. A weapon **SO POWERFUL** that it would change the world forever with the push of a button . . .

THIS BUTTON!

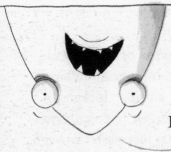

But what's wrong with being
cute and cuddly?
I wish *I* were cute and cuddly!
Everyone **LOVES** guinea pigs.

I don't want *love*,
you ridiculous fish.

I
WANT
POWER.

And now that I have it, there's

NOTHING

any of you can do to take it away
from me!

HEHE
HEHEHE!

Ahhh . . . sorry. Can you
just give us a second?

What?
Um . . . all right.
But don't take long, OK?

OK. So the guinea pig is out of his mind. What do we do?

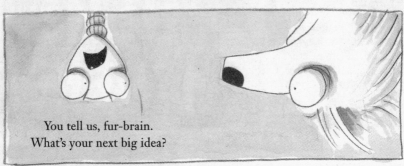

You tell us, fur-brain. What's your next big idea?

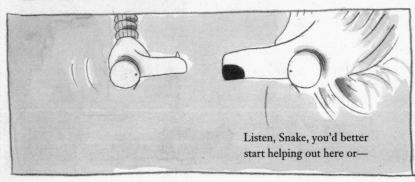

Listen, Snake, you'd better start helping out here or—

OR WHAT?

Guys, cut it out.

OR YOU'LL BE **SORRY**,
YOU NASTY LITTLE
OVERGROWN SLUG!

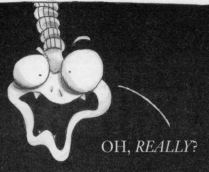

OH, *REALLY*?

AND WHAT ARE YOU GOING TO DO?

ARE YOU GOING TO

BORE ME TO DEATH

WITH YOUR NEXT IDIOTIC PLAN TO
TURN US ALL INTO **GOODY-GOODY
GUMDROPS?!**

**THAT'S
YOUR
LAST
WARNING,
SNAKE.**

You both need to stop arguing. It's starting to really UPSET me . . .

Warning, schmorning! Do your worst, you dimwitted **HERO WANNABE!**

THAT'S IT!

DON'T DO IT, WOLF.

TOO LATE!

MUNCH!

Let me out of here right now!

Hey! Did he just eat the snake?!

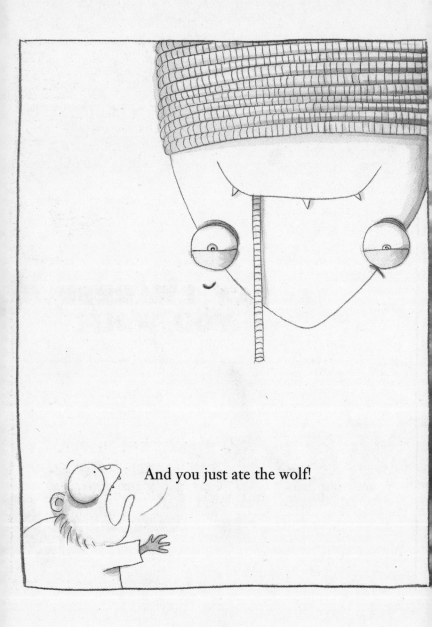

And you just ate the wolf!

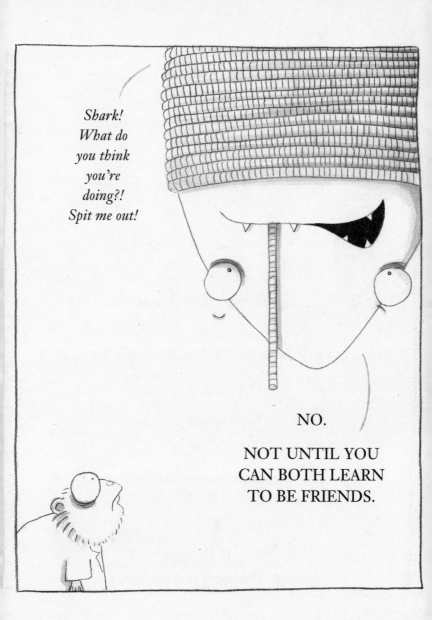

I'm warning you, Wolf! Cough me up!

Not a chance, Slimy.
Shark! I'm NOT going to ask you again!

Wait a minute! Are you inside the shark?!

None of your business!

But that means I'm inside a wolf AND a shark!

Tell someone who cares!

*This is like being trapped inside some kind of really
disgusting nesting doll and I DON'T LIKE IT!*

Big whoop.
Shark, I'm going to count to ten . . .

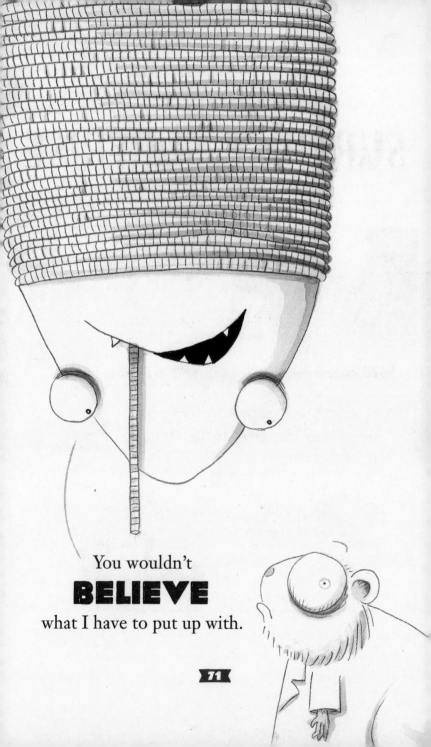

You wouldn't **BELIEVE** what I have to put up with.

71

· CHAPTER 5 ·
SURPRISE, SURPRISE

Oh, man! There are guards everywhere!
How are we ever going to find them?

Hey, look!
Down there!

It's Shark!

NO ONE TIES UP MY
CHICOS AND GETS
AWAY WITH IT!
LET'S CUT THAT ROPE
RIGHT NOW!

NIBBLE!

NIBBLE!
NIBBLE!

Mr. Piranha?

Yeah, kid?
What is it?

NIBBLE!
NIBBLE!

I know this sounds crazy . . .
but I really do think
I saw a ninja.

Oh, man. You must have hit your
head *hard, hermano*. There's no
such thing as ninjas. They only exist
in fairy-tale stories, like *Snow White
and the Seven Samurai*.

Actually,
I'm pretty
sure that's
not true . . .

FREEZE!

Oh no!

SHARK! I'm sorry! They caught us!

Piranha?! Is that you?

Oh, yes. I forgot to mention—your silly little friends thought they could sneak in here and rescue you! Isn't that *adorable*?

It seems that none of you fully understand how much danger you're in.

Oh well. I guess I'll just

UNLEASH THE END OF THE WORLD AS WE KNOW IT!

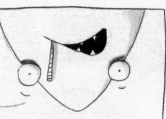

If you don't mind me saying, you seem like a very troubled guinea pig.

You have NO idea.

NOW LET'S GET THIS PARTY STARTED!

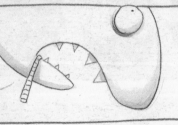

PIRANHA! RUN!

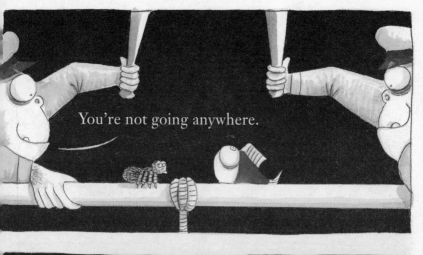

You're not going anywhere.

Hmmm.
Sorry,
gentlemen,
but I think
you might be
wrong about
that one.

What did I tell you?!

SLICE!!

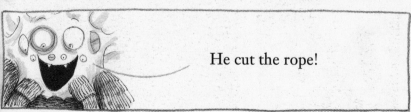

He cut the rope!

SPLAT!

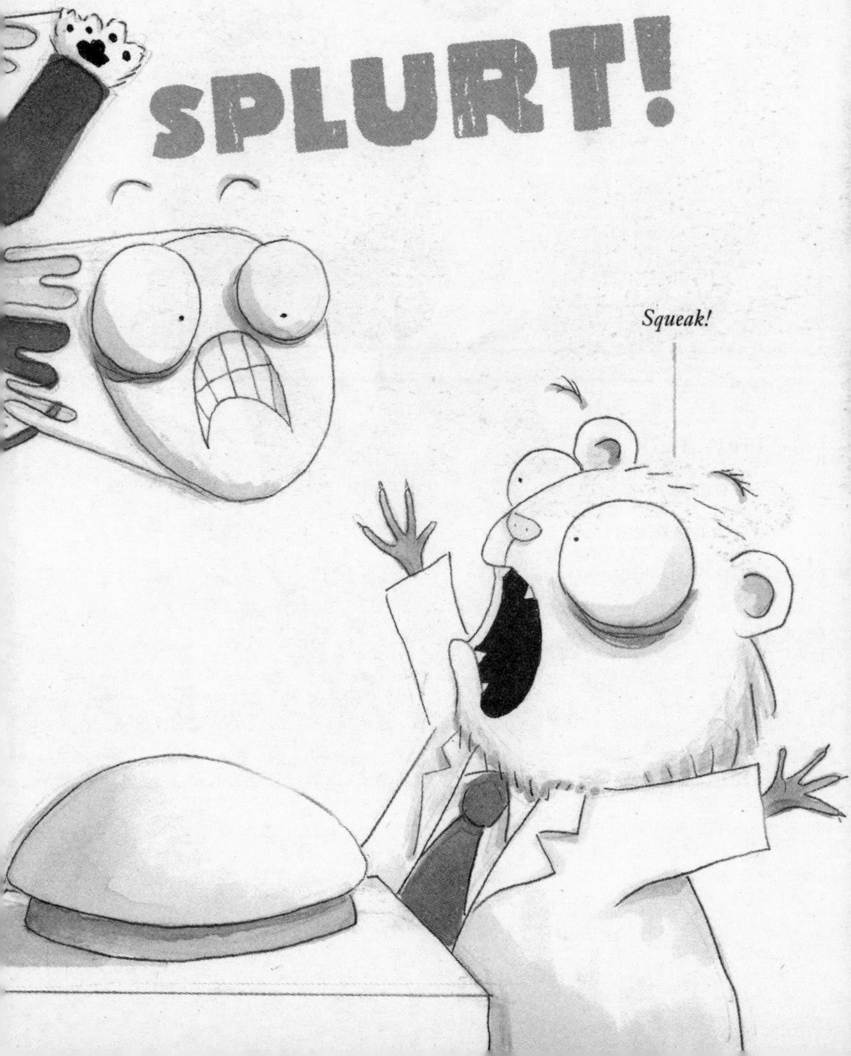
SPLURT!
Squeak!

Hey, man.
Thanks.
You broke
my fall.

OK. Does someone want to tell me what's going on here?

Certainly, Mr. Wolf . . .

· CHAPTER 6 ·
the SECRET AGENT

Who **ARE** you?

My name is
SPECIAL AGENT FOX,
Mr. Shark.
And I'm very pleased
to meet you.

I'm afraid you boys have stumbled into a very dangerous situation.

Doctor Rupert Marmalade is one of the most **DESPICABLE VILLAINS** on the face of the earth. We've been on his tail for years, trying to catch him in the act.

It seems we've finally done it.

We? Who's *we*?

I'm an agent for the

INTERNATIONAL LEAGUE OF HEROES.

We're a secret global organization sworn to protect the earth from evil.

And that is what we do.

Hey! That's kind of what *we* do, isn't it, Wolfie?

Wolfie?

What's up with him?

. . . So awesome . . .
. . . so pretty . . .
. . . *guuuhhhhh* . . .
. . . *mhuuuunghhh* . . .

I'm not sure what's happening . . .

Never mind.

We are the . . .
Good Guys Club,
Agent Fox . . .
at your service . . .
heh heh heh . . .
ah . . . yup . . .
gughhhh . . .

The "Good
Guys Club"?
Is that what you
call yourselves?

Yep. We sat up ALL NIGHT
trying to think of the
STUPIDEST NAME in
the HISTORY OF **STUPID**
NAMES and—**BAM!**—
there it was.

Oh, I don't know.
I think it's kind of cute.

But I'm afraid you're a little
out of your depth here, boys.

Your antics at the chicken farm made old Doctor Marmalade here **OBSESSED** with you. But don't worry. We'll soon have him safely locked up, won't we, Marma—

Oh dear.

Has anyone seen where the supervillain went?

Right here, Agent Fox.

Whoops. That's unfortunate.

And I DO hope you enjoy the **END OF THE WORLD!**

He he!

CLUNK!

MY **SECRET WEAPON** HAS BEEN RELEASED AND IT'S **ON ITS WAY!** CAN YOU GUESS WHAT IT IS?

HEHE HE!

Oh, and just to
make things a little
more interesting . . .

FOOF!

THIS BUILDING WILL
SELF-DESTRUCT
IN 90 SECONDS . . .
89! 88!
87! 86!

76! 75! 74! 73!

Hmm. The old disappearing-up-a-great-big-bendy-tube trick. That's disappointing.

Well, the building is about to blow and we have seconds to live. Any ideas, gentlemen?

· CHAPTER 7 ·
LEARNING TO RIDE A BIKE

Climb aboard, everyone, and I'll get you out of here.

We won't all fit on one motorcycle!

Hmm. You could be right. I don't suppose any of you can ride one of these . . . ?

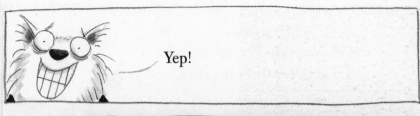

Yep!

You can?

Yeeeah.

Really?

Nnnnn . . . *yeeeeah.*

I just didn't want to disappoint her.

You know what?

What?

Let's just . . .

PUT THE PEDAL TO THE METAL!

Wow. You have a very unusual style, Mr. Wolf. Very impressive.

But I'm afraid things are going to be a little more difficult than we thought.

Oh, really? Why's that?

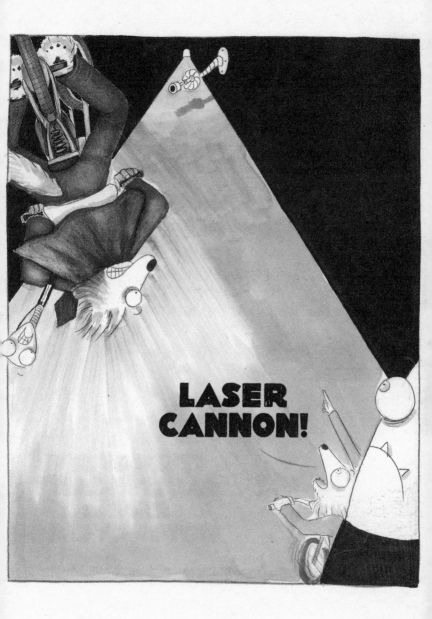

Wow. He really is awfully brave, isn't he?

Well, yes. In Bolivia, we have a name for people like that . . .

We call them "idiots."

I HATE YOU, WOLF!

WELL, I **DON'T** HATE YOU, SNAKE!

AND I **WON'T GIVE UP ON YOU**, NO MATTER WHAT HAPPENS.

I'M SORRY I **ATE** YOU EARLIER. BUT I'M **NOT** SORRY FOR GETTING YOU INTO ALL THIS TROUBLE.

THIS IS WHAT HEROES DO.

AND I TRULY BELIEVE **YOU HAVE A HERO INSIDE YOU**, MR. SNAKE.

AND I'LL NEVER STOP BELIEVING THAT. **EVER**.

You're crazy. And you're going to get us all killed.

MAYBE!

BUT NOT TODAY!

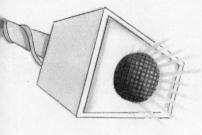

THIS BUILDING WILL SELF-DESTRUCT IN 10 SECONDS . . . 9! 8! 7! 6! 5!

Everyone take cover!

4!

3!

2!

1!

· CHAPTER 8 ·
A LITTLE FAVOR

What happened?
Did we blow up?
Is this . . . heaven?

It can't be.
You're here.

HEHEHEHE!

Tricked you!
The building wasn't
REALLY going to blow up!

Are you kidding?!
I nearly pooped my pants!

Again?!
You really need to
see a doctor, man.

YOU DIDN'T
REALLY THINK
I'D BLOW UP MY
**SECRET
WEAPON**,
DID YOU?

I'm getting sick of this.
WHAT secret weapon?
I'll bet it's just another trick!

Hmmm.
Well, you just wait a few minutes,
Mr. Wolf, and see what comes out
of this tunnel!

YOU believe me, don't you, Agent Fox?

Unfortunately, yes, I do.

What have you done this time, Marmalade?

You'll see.
Well, good luck, everyone.
You're going to need it.

TODAY IS
THE END OF
CUTE AND
CUDDLY . . . .
FOREVER!

I really don't like that guinea pig.

Nor do I, Mr. Wolf.
And that's why I need
to ask you a favor.

Anything!

I need to follow
Marmalade
RIGHT NOW.
But someone
needs to stay here
and deal with his
**SECRET
WEAPON**.

Any minute now, something **TRULY TERRIFYING** will come out of that tunnel and I need some heroes to be standing guard when it does.

Will **YOU** be my heroes, gentlemen?

Will you help me
SAVE THE WORLD?

Um . . . I'm really not sure . . .

I actually have a hair
appointment to get to . . .

I'd love to help, *señorita*, but I'm afraid
I need to find a clean pair of pants . . .

Sister, you're out of your mind . . .

OF COURSE WE WILL!

Thank you, Mr. Wolf.
I'm counting on you, boys.

We all are.

Oh great.
Now she's counting on us.

Well, I've got a villain to catch!

She's even got **ROCKET BOOTS!**

Yes, there are quite a few perks to being a hero, Mr. Wolf.

Oh, and Mr. Snake?

Yeah?

I know what you did at the chicken farm. **YOU** are the reason those chickens are free. You're ALREADY a hero.

You just have to start *believing* it.

Good luck, boys!

ZOOOOM!

• CHAPTER 9 •
CUTE AND CUDDLY NO MORE

Did you hear that?

Yeah. There's something
moving around in there . . .

Are you guys ready for this?

NO.

Fair enough.
I'm not sure I am either.
But it doesn't matter,
does it? Because we have
a job to do. It's up to us
to protect the world.

It's up to us—
**THE GOOD
GUYS CLUB.**

Seriously, man, now that we've heard about the **INTERNATIONAL LEAGUE OF HEROES**, our name sounds so lame it makes me wish I had hands—so I could **SLAP YOU**.

Really?
You don't like our name?

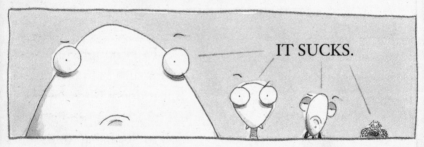

IT SUCKS.

OK . . . well . . .
We **ARE** helping the awesome League of Heroes, right now . . .

So that kind of makes us awesome, too, doesn't it?

Kind of.

Well then, Kind-of-Awesome-League-of-Good-Guys-Guys, let's show this SECRET WEAPON what we're made of!

Hey! **HAHAHAHA!**
Everybody relax!
LOOK!
IT'S JUST ANOTHER **TRICK!**
IT'S JUST A BUNCH OF . . .

Phew!
Well, **THAT'S** a relief!

No, no, no . . . wait a minute . . .
There's something **WEIRD**
about those kittens.
Why are they **LIMPING?**
And **MOANING?**
And . . . **DROOLING?**

NO!
IT CAN'T BE!
IT IS!
IT'S . . .
IT'S AN ARMY
OF . . .

It's a ZOMBIE KITTEN APOCALYPSE!

Should you **panic**? Should you **cry**?

Should you **poop your pants**?

NO! You should sit back and watch the **FUR FLY** as the world's **BADDEST GOOD GUYS** take on **MAD MARMALADE'S MEOWING MONSTERS!**

You'll **laugh till you cry**. Or **laugh till you fart**. (It doesn't matter which, it's totally your choice.)

Just don't miss . . . *the* **BAD GUYS** *in Attack of the Zitten*

AARON BLABEY

THE BAD GUYS

EPISODE 4   **ATTACK OF THE ZITTENS**

(GOOD)

ZOMBIE KITTEN INVASION!

ATTACK OF THE ZITTENS

Good evening.

If there's anyone
still out there, please
listen carefully . . .

TIFFANY FLUFFIT

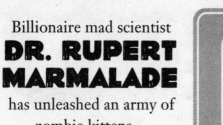

Billionaire mad scientist **DR. RUPERT MARMALADE** has unleashed an army of zombie kittens—commonly known as **ZITTENS** ...

MARMALADE: THE FACE OF EVIL

and **NO ONE IS SAFE!**

CR ASH!

Even this television station has been **SURROUNDED**. I'm not sure how much longer we'll be on the air, but I'll tell you what we know . . .

The Zittens are furry and super-cute but **ABSOLUTELY DEADLY**.

Make no mistake, they will **TRY TO EAT YOU!** But here are a few things that may help you escape . . .

TOP TIPS FOR SURVIVING THE KITTEN APOCALYPSE

First, many of them wear **LITTLE BELLS**. IF YOU HEAR A CUTE LITTLE BELL—

RUN AND HIDE!

Second, they **DO NOT LIKE WATER**. Water is your best **DEFENSE**. It really annoys them and can sometimes make them go away.

And finally, they are easily distracted by **BALLS OF YARN**. If you come across a Zitten, tossing them a ball of yarn is your best chance of **ESCAPE**.

However,
if you encounter a
**WHOLE LITTER
OF ZITTENS**,
none of this
will help you.

THIS ISN'T GOOD!

If you are attacked by a litter,
there is only one thing you can do—

**RUN AS FAST
AS YOU CAN!**

CRASH!

Oh no! They're inside!

MEEEEOOOORGWW!

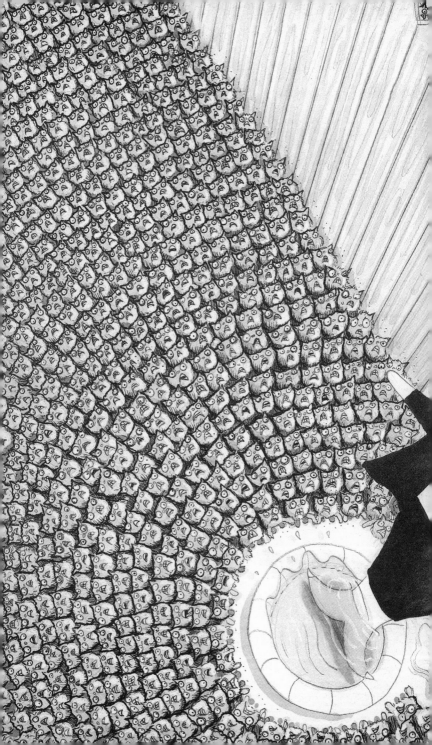

Just remember— it could be worse . . .

WORSE?!

OK, that's it. I say we throw them the wolf so the rest of us can make a run for it.

Stop moving around!
You're making the
water splash out of the
kiddie pool!

Yeah, cut it out, Mr. Snake! That water is the only thing between us and those tiny flesh-eating monsters!

Well, *you'd* know all about **TINY FLESH-EATING MONSTERS**, wouldn't you?

Like you can talk, **MR. I-EAT-MICE-AND-ANY-OTHER-CUTE-LITTLE-FAMILY-PETS!**

Cut it out, guys! Don't forget who we are— WE'RE THE

GOOD GUYS CLUB!

Seriously?! *Again* with that stupid name?

Sorry—I mean . . . we're the **SORT-OF-INTERNATIONAL-LEAGUE-OF-HEROES-TYPE-GUYS**, and we'd never run away from a fight like this, would we?

We *can't* run away, *hermano*.
We're surrounded.

And maybe that's a
GOOD thing!

WHAT?!

Well . . . this gives us another chance to be awesome, doesn't it?

OK. I've changed my mind. Let's throw them the wolf.

No, no, listen! **DR. MARMALADE**, that rotten little billionaire guinea pig, created this army of Zittens for one reason and one reason only . . .

What reason?

So that we can defeat them and say **"IN YOUR FACE, DR. MARMALADE!"**

Actually, you know what, guys? I'm with you. Let's throw them the wolf.

No, wait!
I think I hear
something . . .

Don't try to
protect him.
Mr. Wolf needs to
"go be a hero" one
last time . . .

Hush up, Slimy.
What do you hear, Legs?

It sounds like . . .

Like what?

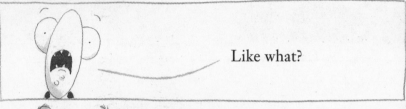

. . . like . . .

LIKE WHAT?!

Does it sound like the claws of a zombie kitten *poking a hole in our kiddie pool*?!

POP!

No. It sounds more like . . .

It's Agent Fox!

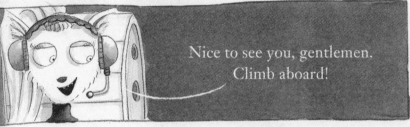

Nice to see you, gentlemen. Climb aboard!

She saved us again!

Yeah. Saved by a girl. *Twice*. This is getting embarrassing.

Embarrassing?!
What's wrong
with you, *chico*?
We're lucky to
know such a strong,
powerful *señorita*!

Yes. We. Are . . .

Oh, pleasssssse . . .

Oh. One
small thing,
Mr. Wolf . . .

Anything!

Would you mind grabbing one of those Zittens for me? That'd be marvelous.

Oh. Uhhhhh . . . sure.

Um . . . OK.

Here, kitty, kitty, kitty.

Anything for you, Agent Fox . . .

RRREEOOOWW!

POUNCE!

Uh-oh.

Did he get one, Mr. Piranha?

EEEEEEEEE

Ah, yes, *señorita*. I think he's just calming it down with a . . . cuddle.

· CHAPTER 2 ·
TWO PLACES AT ONCE

eeegggaarrhhhh!

It bit my nose!
I'M GOING TO TURN INTO A ZOMBIE!

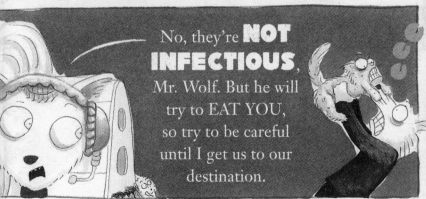

No, they're **NOT INFECTIOUS**, Mr. Wolf. But he will try to EAT YOU, so try to be careful until I get us to our destination.

eee

Oh! What a **relief—a**

aaaaarrhhhh!

What destination? Where are we going?

Legs? Can you take the controls?

You got it!

Gentlemen, I know someone who might
be able to help with this Zitten situation.
Her name is

GRANNY GUMBO,

and if we can bring her a live Zitten,
there's a chance she can create an

ANTIDOTE

and turn them all
back into
normal kittens.

An antidote? Well, that sounds **tremend—**

Unfortunately, it's not that simple.

It never is.

I need to get this Zitten to **GRANNY GUMBO**.

But I *also* need to keep following

DR. MARMALADE.

Trouble is—I can't be
in two places at once.

So, Mr. Shark?

And Mr. Piranha?

Yeah?

I need your help.

Why us?

Because you two can **SWIM**.

I've managed to track Marmalade to an island

fifty miles off the coast of **COSTA RICA**.

I need you to swim out there, in secret,

and keep an eye on him.

And I hope you don't mind,

but I would recommend wearing

a **DISGUISE**.

Mind? You just made my day. I'm in.

Um . . .

Mr. Piranha? You seem troubled. Is everything OK?

Uh, I might have a slight problem, *señorita* . . .

What?

I'm a freshwater fish.

So?

I'm not supposed to swim in the ocean. It can be really bad for my tummy.

Are you kidding?! What is the point of a fish that won't go in the water?

I'm not saying I won't.
I'm just not a big fan of
salt water, *hermano*.

YOU'RE A *FISH*!

I'm a *FRESHWATER* fish!

So, let me get this straight—you and
Moby Dick over here *WALK AROUND* like
it's the most normal thing in the world,
but you're worried about getting

A LITTLE SALT IN
YOUR GILLS?!

Hmm, I was actually
wondering how you
manage to walk around
so much myself . . .

. . . not that it's any of
my business . . .

Don't worry, Piranha.
I'll get you to that island
safely. And just for the
record—if we want to
walk around . . .

THAT'S IT!
I'M GONNA EAT THAT UGLY SON OF A CATERPILLAR!

Heeeey! Take it easy, fellas. Agent Fox can hear you. Try to be a little bit cool, will **YOU**–

–oooooohhhhh, my face! It's. Got. My. Face!

Yeah. Sure, Wolf. We'll try to be cool. Just like you.

EEEEEEE

Legs? Take us lower.
Mr. Shark? This is your stop.
And Mr. Piranha?
It's your choice . . .

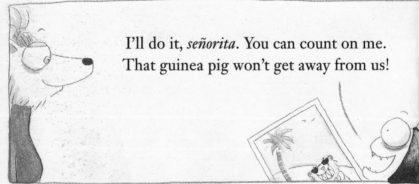

I'll do it, *señorita*. You can count on me.
That guinea pig won't get away from us!

Good for you, Piranha.
I'll be thinking of you.
And I sure hope you
don't get a-**SALT**-ed!

OOOOOOH! I'M GOING TO TEACH YOU A LESSON, YOU ROTTEN LITTLE BAG OF—

Sure. He's an idiot.
But he's *our* idiot.

· CHAPTER 3 ·
GRANNY

I hear you, Agent Fox . . .

Legs? Stay close. I'll contact you when it's time to pick us up.

Stay safe, guys.

Thanks, Legs. But . . . Agent Fox?

This is **GRANNY GUMBO'S WAREHOUSE**. Now, I should warn you— Granny is a *little* bit . . . odd. So you might want to leave the talking to me . . .

Yeah, yeah, whatevs. Hey, look, it's open . . . YO! OLD LADY! WHERE'S THE MILK AND COOKIES?

GRAB!

Well, look what's makin' a ruckus in my parlor! A sweet, tasty

GRUB!

Yumitty YUM YUM YUM! I'm gonna eat you UP!

Oh dear . . .

Oh, you sure are
gonna taste goo . . .

goo . . . gaah . . . gAAAH . . .

AAAAHHH...

AAAAAA AHHHHH...

GRAB!

Bless you, Granny.

Who's *that*?
Is that you,
Miss Fox?
I do declare!

But what are you doin' bringing a flea-bitten **MUTT-DOG** into my parlor?! You know I'm allergic to mutt-dogs!

I do apologize, Granny. But I was rather hoping . . .

Oh, never you mind, 'cause you brought me a sweet treat, too!

Wait a
minute!
Where's
my teeth?

On my face, Granny.

Give me back my choppers, Mutt-Dog.

Granny?
I'm sorry to interrupt,
but do you remember when
we talked about finding a

ZOMBIE KITTEN ANTIDOTE?

Antidote?
What antidote? Oh!
For *this* thing?!

OF COURSE I REMEMBER!

I've got my special brew cookin' right now, as a matter of fact . . .

Marvelous, Granny.

Now, I just need a pinch of his **FUR** . . .

SPRINKLE!
SPRINKLE!

But where am I going to find me some snake bite venom at this hour . . . ?

Well . . .

Wolf! Don't you dare . . .

Hush your mouth, Grub. What's that you're sayin', Mutt-Dog?

I think you'll find all the venom you need right there in that . . . grub, Granny.

Well, I do declare! I believe you're right—this mean-eyed, low-down snake in the grass will do *nicely* . . .

Now you
listen to me—

HUSH, child.
And hold still.

Wait a minute,
lady. *Have you
been professionally
trained by a vet to
extract venom?!*

· CHAPTER 4 ·
the MASTER OF DISGUISE

OK. Open your eyes . . .

Uhhh . . .
OK. I give up.
Why are you dressed
like a unicorn?

What?! Oh. Sorry. Hang on . . .
Let me change the angle . . .

TA-DA!

Ohhhhhh! I get it!
You're a **DOLPHIN!**
Man, you are SO good
at disguises.

No, no, no, no!
Why are you **NAKED**, *chico*?!

When was the last
time you saw a dolphin
wearing clothes?

Well . . . never.
But you've been spending
too much time with
that bare-butt spider,

LEGS,

that's what *I* think . . .

Build a bridge and GET OVER IT, little buddy. I'm as free as a dolphin and **LOVING IT!**

I know I'm going to regret asking this, but why do you have **A BOWL** on your head, *chico*?

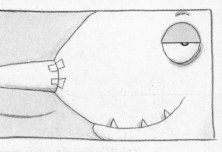

Because THIS little dolphin has a pet goldfish named Mindy.

I hope you're not saying what I think you're saying . . .

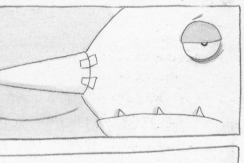

Get in the fishbowl, Mindy.

Are you out of your mind?! You want me to pretend to be a goldfish named Mindy?!

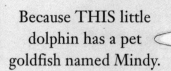

Now you're getting it.
When I'm finished with you, **NO ONE**
will recognize us. We'll find Marmalade, and
YOU won't get a drop of salt water on you.

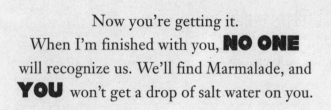

I refuse to be naked,
chico! I won't do it!

Calm down and
put this on. We're
running out of time.

MOMENTS LATER . . .

This is so humiliating, man. No one is going to believe this getup . . .

Oh yeah?

Hey, guys! I'm really excited to take my pet goldfish, Mindy, to see

THIS ISLAND

with a creepy guinea pig on it, but I'm not sure where it is. You don't know how to find it, do you?

Oh, I do!

So do I!
We can
take you
there!

C'mon, friend! Follow us!

C'mon, Mindy!
This'll be fun!

· CHAPTER 5 ·
the ANTIDOTE

Wha . . . ?

What happened?

Hello, Mr. Snake. I'm glad to see you're feeling better. It was very kind of you to donate some venom. Granny really appreciates it.

DONATE?! She just **CLOBBERED** me with a frying pan! She's completely *insane*!

Whoa, there! Take it easy, good buddy. I'm sure Agent Fox knows what she's doing . . .

Oh, well, if YOU say so, you **LOVE-STRUCK BUFFOON**, then it MUST be true!

Actually, perhaps we could get Granny to clobber him just one more time, *heh heh heh* . . .

I must apologize for Granny. Her methods are **HIGHLY UNUSUAL**, but I promise you, Mr. Snake— she is a genius.

Oh, really? Is that why she's got her head up a roast turkey's butt?

Good gracious! Where'd everybody go?! I can't see . . .

AAHHH . . . AAAHHHHH . . .

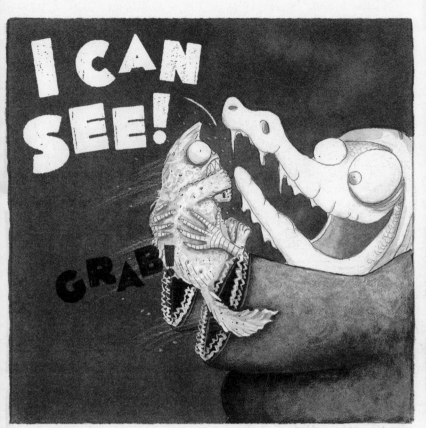

Oh yeah. She's a genius, all right.

Hush your mouth, Grub, and pass me one of them balls of yarn. It's time for the Granny Gumbo Show!

Wow! Why do you have so much yarn, Granny?

I make it from the hair of all the mutt-dogs I **EAT**.

I thought you were allergic to . . . mutt-dogs . . .

Yeah, but they taste so GOOD, I can't help myself.

Brilliant. Now we're going to die in here with this toothless lunatic.

Hold it together, gentlemen. Granny? It's time . . .

I hear you! Mutt-Dog, **CATCH!**

SPLAT! AARGGH!

Now watch this . . .

DUNK!

HERE, KITTY!

Oh my stars! It actually works!

You *are* a genius, Granny!

FART!

What did you say?

I'm sorry to poop on your party, but if we walk out there, those things will tear us to pieces before we toss even one ball of wool. There's just **TOO MANY OF THEM . . .**

I say we load up the

BIG BOY

and take him for a spin.
Whaddya say?

· CHAPTER 6 ·
TROUBLE ON GUINEA PIG ISLAND

Here's the island, guys!
Isn't it *awesome*?

Wow. These dolphins
are so cute and friendly!

Yeah.

I still feel weird that they're all nude, though. We don't do skinny-dipping in Bolivia, *hermano*.

I know. It's an ocean thing. You'll get used to it. Can you see anything yet?

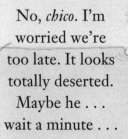

No, *chico*. I'm worried we're too late. It looks totally deserted. Maybe he . . . wait a minute . . .

LOOK!

MARMALADE!

What's he doing up there?
That looks like a . . .

Hey, guys!
Let's play a game!

Yeah!
Let's see who
can jump the
highest!

I can't see him. This isn't good.

Man, I thought dolphins were supposed to be smart . . .

That's just a myth. Some of them are really stupid.

I love jumping!

Let's jump some more!

So what do we do now? Should we go up there and look for him?

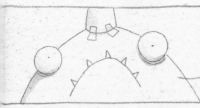 Uh-oh. Somehow I don't think we need to . . .

 *¡Ay, caramba!*

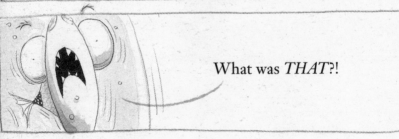 What was *THAT*?!

So where do
you suppose
he's going . . . ?

CHAPTER 7

KEEP ON TRUCKIN'

ANNY GUMBO'S
L-NATURAL HERBS & POTIONS

OK, gentlemen.
Are we ready to go?

Nearly! I just need to
tighten these pillows . . .

What are you
doing, Wolf?

We're GOOD GUYS,
remember? We don't want
to HURT any kittens.
We want to **SAVE**
all the kittens.

These **CUSHIONS**
and **PILLOWS**
will make sure that none
of them gets hurt . . . as we
plow through them at
high speed.

Yeah.

That's the stupidest thing I've ever heard. You've made a perfectly cool truck look ridiculous.

That's just one snake's opinion. I think it looks great.

If by "great" you mean "dumb," then yes—it looks "great."

Quit your yappin' and get up here! It's time to hit the road!

Remember, boys— I'll **DRIVE THE TRUCK**, you **THROW THE YARN**. There are **THOUSANDS** of Zittens so this isn't going to be easy, but if anyone can do it, we can.

You're so awesome! I mean . . . I just love you . . . I mean . . . I think you're the coolest . . . I mean . . . yeah . . . no . . . yeah.

And the winner of the most embarrassing speech award goes to . . .

Don't listen to him, Mr. Wolf. I think you're **GREAT.**

OK, boys. Let's roll . . .

Dunk and throw, varmints! Dunk and throw!

Oh man . . .
there's
MILLIONS
of them!

Boys? Can you hear me?

Yes, Agent Fox. What can we do for you?

The Zittens are spread out wider than we thought. We need to find a way to **THROW THE YARN FARTHER**.

Oh yeah?
And how do
you suggest
we do that?

Don't worry,
Agent Fox.
I'll think of
something.
You look lovely
today,
by the way . . .

Thank you,
Mr. Wolf.

Oh **BARF!**

**WOLF AND FOX!
SITTING IN A TREE!**

K! I! S-S! I-N-G!

Shhh!

STUFF!

Wait a minute.
That gives me . . .

. . . an
IDEA!

VOOOOOM!

That's IT! Whatever you're doing, Mr. Wolf, keep it up!

Oh, no you don't! You're not going to use me as a **CATAPULT** again! I forbid it! I—

STUFF! STUFF! STUFF!

Nonsense! This is your moment to **SHINE**, little buddy.

The question is—how many balls of yarn does it take to stuff a snake?

Quite a few, as it turns out.

Ooooooh! Look at that **BIG JUICY GRUB!** He's makin' me feel a bit peckish . . .

Hey, kitties . . .

That's brilliant, Mr. Wolf!

YOU'VE DONE IT!

WOO-HOO!

NOTHING

can stop us now!

Hmmm . . .

MUNCH!

Hey! *WHERE'S SNAKE?!*

In my **BELLY**,
Mutt-Dog,
oh yes indeedie!

*Wolf! Get me
out of here!*

You ate
Snake?!
What is *wrong*
with you?

I'm **HUNGRY**, that's what. And I'm fixin' to eat me some **MUTT-DOG**, tooooo . . .

ooo . . .
oooh . . .
ahh . . .
AHHHH . . .

. . . **CHOO!**

BONK!

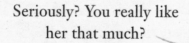

AGENT FOX!

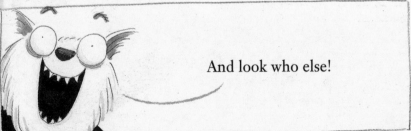

And look who else!

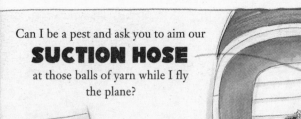

Can I be a pest and ask you to aim our **SUCTION HOSE** at those balls of yarn while I fly the plane?

Sounds good to me!

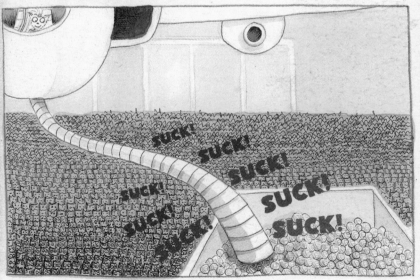

SUCK! SUCK! SUCK! SUCK! SUCK! SUCK! SUCK! SUCK! SUCK!

OK, that should do it. Now . . . let's put a stop to this nonsense, shall we?

· CHAPTER 8 ·
the BAD PENNY

Hi, everybody!

Listen carefully because I have a special, private message— just for **YOU!** Aren't you lucky? First of all, congratulations on surviving **PHASE ONE** of my little plan.

11:09

SHOPPING CE

Phase One?! I don't like the sound of this . . .

Sure, a few kittens is one thing.

But imagine if I had a weapon SO powerful that it

could turn **EVERY CUTE AND CUDDLY CREATURE ON THE PLANET** into a **DROOLING WEAPON OF DESTRUCTION!**

Wouldn't that just be **AWESOME?!**

He's lying! He doesn't have a weapon like that! That's impossible . . .

Is it? Well, let me introduce you to the CUTE-ZILLA RAY, Mr. Wolf!

Just imagine a world where every puppy . . .

bunny . . .

pony . . .

and dolphin . . .

. . . could be changed,
just by pulling one
little lever . . .

INTO AN **EVIL**, DIABOLICAL, TOTALLY OFFENSIVE...

ZUPPY!

ZUNNY!

ZONY!

OR ZOLPHIN!

C'mon, Mindy! Let's get out of here!

Stop calling me Mindy!

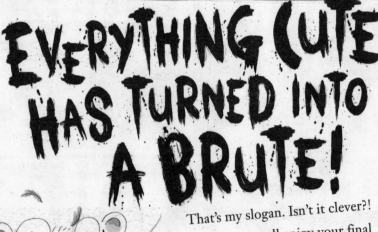

EVERYTHING CUTE HAS TURNED INTO A BRUTE!

That's my slogan. Isn't it clever?! I hope you all enjoy your final day on Earth. Oh, and to the

INTERNATIONAL LEAGUE OF HEROES . . .

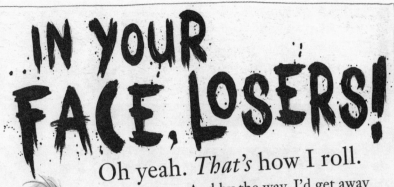

...IN YOUR FACE, LOSERS!

Oh yeah. *That's* how I roll.

And by the way, I'd get away

from those kittens if I were you.

Because no antidote

ON EARTH

will help you

this time . . .

RREEOOWW! RREEOOWW!

Well, that's all from me, funsters.
So . . .

SEE YA!
Wouldn't wanna **BE YA!**

And they call
ME crazy!

SHOPPING

· CHAPTER 9 ·
A BIT FARTHER THAN EXPECTED

Chico! We're done for!

NO! LOOK!

Good to see
you, guys!

Legs! Get us out of here!

Chicos!
Thank you, my
friends! But
listen—everyone
is in danger.
Marmalade
took off in a
ROCKET,
and our dopey
little dolphin
buddies turned
into monsters
and . . .

But how?
We don't even know where the
CUTE-ZILLA RAY is.

I think I
might know.

Legs?

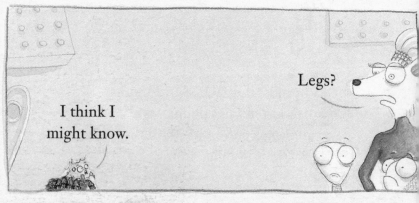

Well, the only way he'd
be able to use it over the
**WHOLE
PLANET**
is if he's beaming
it in from
SPACE ...

We saw him leave the planet in a rocket . . .

OK. Well, there's only one place he can land, isn't there?

Oh, Legs. You're right. The only way we can find him and destroy that weapon is to get to . . .

Where? Where do
we have to get?

Mr. Piranha, we have to get to . . .

TO BE CONTINUED . . . .

THE BAD NEWS? The world is ending.
THE GOOD NEWS?
The **BAD GUYS** are back to **save it!**

Sure, they might have to "borrow" a **rocket** . . .

And there might be something **NASTY** in one

of the **space suits** . . . And Mr Piranha *miiiiight*

have eaten too many **bean burritos** . . .

But seriously, how **BAD** can it be?

How bad?! **SUPER BAD.** It's one small

step for the **Sort-of-International-League-of-Good-Guys guys.**

It's one giant leap for

the **BAD GUYS** in

Intergalactic Gas!